Coyote Claus:

A
Southwestern
Desert
Tale

Written by
Cory Cooper Hansen

Artwork by
Mark A. Hicks

Sunbelt Publications, Inc.
San Diego, California

DEDICATIONS

To my dad, whose spirit joins me as I hike Sonoran trails. And to Stan,
who turned me around to experience the desert in a new and wonderful way. —C.C.H

To the magic of the desert night. May it be preserved unspoiled
for future generations to experience its wonder. —M.A.H.

Coyote Claus: A Southwestern Desert Tale

Sunbelt Publications, Inc.
Text Copyright © 2019 by Cory Cooper Hansen
Illustrations Copyright © 2019 by Mark A. Hicks
All rights reserved. First edition 2019

Illustrations and book layout by Mark A. Hicks
Cover and book production by Kristina Filley
Project management by Deborah Young
Printed in China

Sunbelt Publications, Inc.
P.O. Box 191126
San Diego, CA 92159-1126
(619) 258-4911, fax: (619) 258-4916
www.sunbeltpublications.com

22 21 20 19   4 3 2 1

'Twas the night before Christmas
And all through the land
Desert creatures were stirring
In Sonoran sand.

The Sonoran Desert is the hot and dry region that stretches between southeastern California, southwestern Arizona, and down into Mexico.

The agave blooms opened
In the cool night air
In hopes that the bats
Soon would be there.

Agave plants can bloom as early as Christmas Eve in the southernmost tip
of the Sonoran Desert. Bats and bees pollinate their blossoms.

The tortoise were nestled
All snug in their beds
While visions of prickly pear
Danced in their heads.

Desert tortoise hibernate during the cool winter months.
Their favorite food is the prickly pear cactus. They even eat the spines.

And perro in his basket
And I in my bed
Had just settled down
For the long night ahead.

**Many people who live in the Southwest are Spanish speakers.
Perro is the Spanish word for dog.**

When out on the mesa
There arose such a howl
I knew in a moment
Coyote did prowl.

Coyote (ky-oh-tee) is a member of the dog family that lives wild in the desert.
His nighttime howls are the song of the southwest.

Within my adobe
I considered the sound,
Then opened the door
And looked all around.

Adobe homes are made from sun-dried bricks of mud and straw.
They are warm in the winter and cool in the summer.

The moon on the crest
Of the ocotillo
Gave the luster of midday
To objects below.

The ocotillo cactus grows long thin branches that have sharp spines
hiding in its green leaves. Bright red-orange flowers bloom in the spring.

When, what to my wondering
Eyes should show up,
But a desert dog band
With one tiny gray pup.

Baby coyotes are called pups. They live and play in a den until they are around
10 weeks old. Then their mom takes them out to learn about hunting.

With a sly old coyote
So grizzled and lean
I knew in a moment
What the racket did mean.

Coyotes look like middle-sized, light gray or tan dogs but
they look rangier and carry their bushy tails low.

Sharper than cactus
His yip yips they came.
The animals he wanted
He called them by name.

Coyotes use different sounds to communicate.
Sharp yips follow howls and let others know who is in the neighborhood.

Come, come javelina!
Each kangaroo rat!
Here rattler, here rabbit,
Here gecko and bat!

Many Sonoran desert creatures are nocturnal.
They sleep during the day when it is so hot and are active at night.

To the top of the ridge,
To the top of mesquite,
Now howl with me, howl with me,
Howl with me sweet.

The mesquite tree drops pods enjoyed by many desert animals.
People cook with the wood because it burns slowly and gives the food a sweet flavor.

As dry leaves that before
The late monsoons do fly,
When they meet with a
Tumbleweed mount to the sky.

Monsoon rainstorms arrive late in the Sonoran summer.
Plants and animals depend on these sudden storms for much of their water.

So up to the mesa
The creatures they crept.
There's safety in numbers,
They thought with each step.

Mesas are desert hills with long, flat tops. Mesa is a Spanish word that means table.

And then, in a twinkling,
I heard on the trail,
The creatures, still worried,
And one sad little wail.

Coyote is a smart and fast predator. He usually hunts for mammals
but will eat anything, even fruits and vegetable matter.

As I drew in my head
And was turning around,
Down the arroyo
Coyote came with a bound.

The sudden rainstorms of monsoons wash out low areas of the desert.
Dry desert gullies, called arroyos, are left behind.

He was dressed all in fur
From his head to his foot
And his whiskers were shiny
Where his supper was put.

Coyotes use their keen senses to find food and avoid danger.
They listen carefully to hear other animals and use their sharp noses to find food.

He called out once more.
The creatures shook with the noise.
"Come here," howled coyote,
"Come here desert boys."

Coyotes have special areas they call their own.
They mark their territories and howl to tell others where they live.

The javelinas agreed,
Their snouts up in a pack,
"We've too often been
A coyote snack."

Javelinas are wild, pig-like animals that live near mesquite and prickly pear.
They eat, sleep, and forage in packs, leaving a musky odor behind.

The kangaroo rats
Hid behind an old gate
And each told a tale
Of losing a mate.

Kangaroo rats are perfect animals for living in the desert. They can get all the water they need from seeds. They only come out in the cool of the night.

The rattler admitted
His tail was no help.
Rabbit just shuddered
And gave a small yelp.

The quick rattlesnake has dangerous fangs. They don't always rattle before striking!
Cottontail rabbits are plentiful and are seen both night and day.

A gecko claw pointed.
No tail said it all.
But bat said, "Don't worry,"
It's a different call!

Geckos are small lizards with long tails. If a predator grabs its tail,
it falls off, allowing the gecko to escape. Bats spread pollen so cactus fruit can grow.

The small pup implored,
"It's past time I was fed!"
Coyote looked down and
Began unpacking instead.

Father coyotes help feed their pups. They hunt while the mothers
are in the den with the babies and come back with food.

A shrug of his shoulders,
A paw to his head,
Soon gave me to know
They had nothing to dread.

Coyote's slyness has earned him the name "trickster" in Native American folklore.
Many stories of his conniving nature have been told.

He howled not a peep
Just laid out his treats:
Insects and cactus,
What each creature eats.

Cactus feeds the javelinas, kangaroo rats, rabbits, and bats.
Geckos eat insects and rattlesnakes eat small mammals.

And laying his forepaw
Aside of his snout,
A different pitch
Of a howl did come out.

Howling is one way coyotes communicate. Pups are called with a huff.
Young coyotes yelp to play or say "too rough." Barks are warning signs.

The animals of the Southwestern Sonoran Desert have adapted to survive in this harsh environment of extreme temperatures and little water.

Then I heard him exclaim
Ere they loped out of sight,
"Feliz Navidad
And to all a good night."

Feliz Navidad means "Happy Christmas" in Spanish
and is used to share in December celebrations.

Cory Cooper Hansen, Ph.D. worked with children, families, and teachers for 30 years before retiring from Arizona State University. Dr. Hansen is published in both academia and children's literature. She is introducing her grandchildren, Connor and Emily, to the wonders of the Sonoran Desert.

Mark A. Hicks is an award-winning illustrator of books, magazines, greeting cards, and much more. He is a native of Arizona and life-long admirer and artistic renderer of Sonoran Desert flora, fauna, and geography. Please visit his website www.MARKiX.net to learn more about his work.

Sunbelt Publications Recommended Reading

Coloring Plants Used by Desert Indians   Diana Lindsay

This book has 40 key plants that desert Indians primarily living in the Sonora Desert of Southern California, Baja California (Mexico), and Arizona have used for centuries. Many of the same or similar species are found in the Mojave Desert of Southern California, Arizona, Nevada, and Utah, and also in the Great Basin Desert of California, Nevada, and parts of Utah, Oregon, and Idaho.

Coloring Southern California Birds   Wendy Esterly

Enjoy coloring 40 commonly seen birds in southern California including year-round residents and migratory visitors. The book includes an eight page color insert to help with identification. It also includes two charts showing the common and scientific name of each bird, its family, where it can be found, and its food preferences.

Desert Critters Wacky Wisdom: The Lives and Survival Skills of Seven Unique Desert Animals   Carol Stout

Basic life-saving survival skills—can't live without them. Parents teach their offspring, and sometimes the lessons and techniques may seem strange, especially in the animal world. Whatever it takes to stay alive and thrive! Find out how seven different desert animals do it, even though it might seem wacky. It is tried and true wisdom that works!

Life in the Slow Lane: Desert Tortoise Tale (Hardcover & Softcover)   Conrad J. Storad

A charming full-color children's book in delightful rhymed verse and a glossary that reveals fundamental facts about these creatures, their desert home, and the hazards they confront on the razor edge of survival and extinction.

Lizards for Lunch: A Roadrunner's Tale   Conrad J. Storad

Roadrunners are speedy, fearless, and when they do take time out from ruling the desert scrub lands and meadows they call home, they enjoy a tasty snack of...

Nature Adventures! A Guidebook of Nature Facts, Songs, and Hikes in San Diego County   Linda Gallo Hawley

This book is a resource guide for parents, teachers, and children focused on studying the animal and plant species found in San Diego County. It teaches the reader to develop observation skills, to notice signs of wildlife, to enjoy, and connect with the natural world.

Who-o-o's Awake in the Desert   Jenny Holt

A southwest bedtime story. As the desert sun sinks into the west, the desert animals prepare for night. Owl takes her nightly flight observing the evening activities before she makes her way to her nest.

Sunbelt Publications publishes and distributes award-winning books that celebrate the land and its people, encouraging readers to conserve the wonders of the Southwest, California, and Baja California.